HICC

written by
MARCIA VAUGHAN
adapted and illustrated by
JOHN VEEKEN

MONDO

For Whitney Graybill

This edition first published in the United States in 1997 by
MONDO Publishing
By arrangement with MULTIMEDIA INTERNATIONAL (UK) LTD

For information contact:
MONDO Publishing
980 Avenue of the Americas
New York, NY 10018
Visit our website at www.mondopub.com

Manufactured in China
First Mondo printing, October 1996
09 10 11 12   9 8 7 6

ISBN 1-57255-171-2

Origianlly published in Australia in 1987 by Horwitz Publications Pty Ltd
Original development by Robert Andersen & Associates and Snowball Educational

RABBIT'S FACE TURNED PINK	THEN RED	THEN PURPLE.
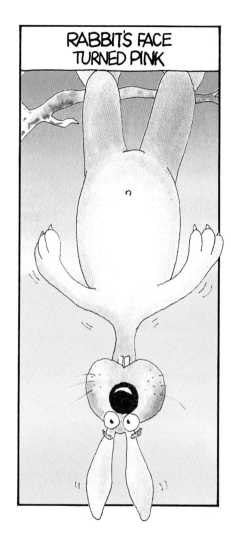		

8

POSSUM SAT
RABBIT ON THE LOG.

SHE SMEARED MUD
ALL OVER HIS FACE.

SHE STUCK TWIGS
BEHIND HIS EARS.

SHE SPRINKLED PEBBLES AND LEAVES ON HIS HEAD.

NOW, TAKE ONE LITTLE SIP FROM THIS PUDDLE.